For Elsa Skeet – AF

For my Foxy friends – EF

STRIPES PUBLISHING
An imprint of Little Tiger Press
1 The Coda Centre, 189 Munster Road,
London SW6 6AW

A paperback original
First published in Great Britain in 2015

ISBN: 978-1-84715-643-3

Fox Investigates

A Whiff of Mystery

ADAM FROST
ILLUSTRATED BY EMILY FOX

Stripes

INVITATION

Adolfo Aroma is proud to launch
his brand-new scent

SMELLISSIMO

Designed for the fox-about-town and the
weasel-who-wants-it-all, the scent combines notes
of musty log with undertones of squashed conkers.

29th August, 6 p.m.

The Grand Ballroom,
The Aroma Mansion, MILAN

WILY SMELLS TROUBLE

Wily Fox, the world's greatest detective, was
in Italy on a very important case. The famous
perfume maker, Adolfo Aroma, was launching
a new scent and he desperately needed Wily's
help. Only a week before, there had been
a mysterious break-in at Adolfo's house.
Nothing had been taken, but Adolfo was
on the alert and he couldn't let anything go
wrong at the launch tonight. He'd called Wily in
to keep a lookout for possible thieves, but Paulo
Polecat, Adolfo's new head of security, was not

5

being very helpful. Wily wanted to look at the guest list, but Paulo insisted it was "top secret".

"You're getting right up my nose," growled Wily.

"Well, you're sticking your nose where it doesn't belong," snarled Paulo.

Adolfo sighed. The rabbit's ears wilted sadly. "Please try to work together, my friends," he said.

Wily stared hard at Paulo. Paulo stared back.

"Fine," said Paulo, and handed Wily a piece of paper.

"Much obliged," Wily muttered.

"Fantastico!" exclaimed Adolfo.

Wily went and found a quiet corner of the room. He looked at the list – there were going to be at least a hundred guests.

He clipped on a headset and started to talk. "Albert, can you hear me?"

"Loud and clear," replied Albert, his voice crackling in Wily's ear.

Albert Mole helped Wily on all his cases. He worked behind the scenes, creating clever gadgets and providing Wily with important information. Right now he was in his secret laboratory underneath Wily's office in London.

"I'm sharing the guest list with you," said Wily. "Does anyone look suspicious?"

Wily held the piece of paper against his smartphone screen until it beeped.

Albert did a quick search. "Just three. Sending you their photos now."

"The first is Bianca Badger," said Albert. "Fashion reporter for the *Pisan Gazette*. Will do anything to get a story. That includes breaking the law."

"She sounds fun."

"Next is Joey Weasel," said Albert. "Former New York gangster. Claims he's now an honest businessman, working in fashion."

"And what about the raccoon?" asked Wily.

"Actually she's a red panda," said Albert. "Rou Red Panda. Owns the biggest fashion and perfume store in China. Hard as nails. Business rivals don't last long."

"Thanks," said Wily. "I'll get the seating plan changed, so they're all sitting near me."

BIANCA   JOEY   ROU

"Hang on, Wily, there's ... that's strange...
Hang up immediately!" Albert gasped. "This line
is no longer secure. I repeat – this line is no
longer secure."

There was a click and then silence. Wily put
away his phone. Someone had been listening in.
But how? Albert was the best in the business –
nobody had managed to tap their calls before.

Adolfo Aroma and Paulo Polecat appeared
behind him.

"Happy with the guest list?" asked Adolfo.

"Sure," said Wily. "I just need to make a
couple of changes to the seating plan..."

It was showtime. The guests were all sitting in rows, chatting happily. At one end of the room there was a stage with a giant glittery SMELLISSIMO banner behind it.

In the first row sat Rou Red Panda, Joey Weasel and Bianca Badger. Wily was seated one row behind them, watching and listening as they talked.

"So, Joey, darling," Bianca drawled, "how are you liking it in fashion?"

"I hear you want to buy Adolfo's business," added Rou.

"Is that right?" Joey replied. "Well, you shouldn't believe everything you read in the papers. Especially hers." He jabbed a furry finger at Bianca.

"For goodness' sake, Joey," sighed Bianca, "everybody knows you'd sell your own mother for a piece of Aroma's empire."

"And everybody knows you'd print any old rubbish to sell newspapers," said Joey.

Their argument was interrupted by a drum roll. The lights went down and a voice boomed from a loudspeaker: "Ladies and gentlemen, may I present ... Adolfo Aroma!"

Pink smoke filled the room and Adolfo appeared, dressed in a top hat and tails.

He was accompanied by a pretty rabbit holding a bottle of aftershave on a cushion.

The audience cheered.

"And now," declared Adolfo, "prepare your noses for the most scintillating scent, the most overwhelming odour, the most sensational smell of your lives. Smellissimo!"

Adolfo removed the cork from the bottle.

Glitter poured down on to the stage. Bianca Badger stood up and started to take photos. Wily glanced round to see if anyone was acting suspiciously – but everything seemed normal.

Until Adolfo and the young rabbit started coughing. Then the front row started to splutter and the perfume maker hit the stage with a thump.

Wily noticed a wisp of yellow smoke coming from the bottle. Then he was hit by the most revolting smell you could imagine. A mixture of old underpants, cowpats and rotten fish.

Everyone started running towards the doors. Rou, Joey and Bianca had all vanished. But Wily couldn't worry about them now – he had to help Adolfo. He breathed in deeply. When he was investigating the Case of the Pirate Penguins, he had managed to hold his breath for four minutes. He might have to do even better now.

Wily pushed his way past upturned chairs and discarded handbags. His chest was getting tighter and his legs were getting weaker, but he kept on going, climbing over a passed-out piglet and an unconscious koala.

He looked up at Adolfo, slumped on the stage. The perfume maker's chest had stopped moving. Wily thought quickly – his legs were starting to buckle, but his arms were still strong. He could use his acrobatic skills.

Wily gritted his teeth, crouched down and leaped through the air, landing on his arms. He pushed himself back up, did two backflips, a triple forward roll and landed right in the middle of the stage.

He picked up the stopper with his mouth, did another forward roll and – still holding the stopper with his teeth – pushed it into the bottle.

Instantly the yellow vapour seemed to disappear.

Wily relaxed and took a big gulp of air. Then he dropped the perfume bottle, kneeled down and tried to get Adolfo breathing again. Almost at once he felt himself being bundled out of the way. It was Paulo Polecat.

"Let me," he growled.

Paulo pushed down on Adolfo's chest until the rabbit spluttered.

"He's going to be OK," said Paulo, with a sigh of relief.

Wily nodded, trying to get his breath back.

"I saw what you did, Fox," said Paulo. "You thought fast and moved even faster. Maybe you are good, after all."

Wily shook his head. "Not that good. I have no idea who did this. Or why."

At that moment, a young rabbit burst into the room.

"Adolfo! Adolfo!" she cried. "It's gone!"

A RECIPE FOR DISASTER

Wily and Adolfo stood staring at the empty safe.

"So what was in there?" asked Wily.

"The secret recipe for Utopia," said Adolfo. "Only one bottle was ever made, by my father. It was presented to Princess Parmigiano on her wedding day. It's the most beautiful scent in the world."

"You perfume guys always say that," said Wily, examining a lump of mud on the floor.

"This time it's true," said Adolfo. "It was my father's greatest achievement. But it had an unfortunate side effect. Everyone who smelled it went into a trance. They just sat there smiling for days – it took one poor mouse a fortnight to snap out of it."

"Incredible," said Wily. "That could cause a lot of trouble in the wrong hands. This break-in you had last week – do you think they were after the recipe?"

"I honestly don't know," said Adolfo.

"Well, at least they left some clues this time," said Wily, pointing to a paw print on the carpet. "Central pad, five fingers, claws. Tooth marks round the safe – powerful canines. We're dealing with a mustelid – otters, ferrets, weasels, red pandas, that kind of thing."

"Well, let's stop every … er … muscle-lid out there and search them!" said Adolfo.

"That's what Paulo's doing," said Wily.

At that moment, Paulo Polecat walked in.

"I've searched everyone from head to toe," he said proudly. "No one's got the recipe."

"I'm glad to see you two are working together at last," said Adolfo.

"Humph," said Paulo, frowning. "Well, it's an emergency, isn't it?"

There was a flash behind them. Wily and Paulo both spun round.

Bianca Badger appeared in the doorway, holding up her smartphone. She was followed by Rou Red Panda and Joey Weasel.

"So, Adolfo," said Bianca, "do you think you'll be able to recover from this disaster?"

"I-I don't wish to talk to the press right now," stammered Adolfo.

"If you want to sell your business, my offer is still on the table," said Joey, with a grin.

"Will Smellissimo still be available in stores on Monday?" asked Rou. "Because I have to say, the recipe needs a little work."

"Obviously that wasn't Smellissimo," groaned Adolfo. "The bottle was switched."

"Yes, and everyone in this room is a suspect," said Wily. "After all, each one of you could benefit from this situation."

Bianca, Rou and Joey took a step backwards.

"Are you saying that one of *us* is responsible?" huffed Bianca.

"Not yet," said Wily, "but when we find out who did this, we will lock them away for a very long time."

Paulo jostled Rou, Bianca and Joey out of the room.

"Do you think it was one of them?" asked Adolfo.

"I'm not sure," said Wily thoughtfully. "And it's not certain that the two crimes are connected. Let's start with the theft of the Utopia recipe. Who would want to create a perfume that dangerous? And why? One thing I'm sure of is that whoever stole the recipe will try to make the perfume. And for that they'll need ingredients. So what *are* the ingredients? Special flowers? Rare herbs? We need to go to where they are grown or sold and see who buys them."

"Ah," murmured Adolfo, his ears drooping. "I'm sorry, Mr Fox, but my memory's not what it was. I'm afraid I can't remember."

"Oh dear," said Wily.

"But … I still have my magnificent nose!" said Adolfo, twitching it happily. "If I had a sample of Utopia, I could tell you what it contained."

"Well, you said Princess Parmigiano has the only bottle," said Wily. "Sounds like I need to pay her a visit. And while I'm gone, perhaps you can find out what was in that stinky bottle. The one that knocked everyone out."

Adolfo nodded. "Good thinking, Mr Fox. Please tell Paulo to bring me the bottle on your way out."

As Wily walked off, he clipped on his headset. "Albert, is the line secure now?"

"Yes, go ahead," Albert replied.

"I'm off to Venice," Wily said. "Send me all the information you can about Princess Parmigiano."

"Will do," said Albert.

Wily reached the hallway of Adolfo's house. A few animals were still making their way out past Paulo, who was standing by the front door.

"I got rid of those three troublemakers," said the polecat.

"Good work," said Wily. "I'm off to Venice, but let me know if anything suspicious happens here." Paulo nodded. "And could you give that bottle of stinky stuff to Adolfo? He's going to work out what was in it."

"Er … um…" Paulo stammered.

"What is it?" asked Wily.

"It's gone," said Paulo, looking embarrassed.

"Gone?" said Wily.

"By the time I came back in here, it had vanished," said Paulo. "But it doesn't matter, does it? What use is that foul-smelling gunk to anyone?"

Wily frowned. "It's called covering your tracks," he said. "And our villain seems to be very good at it." He patted Paulo on the back. "But don't worry. I'll soon sniff them out."

WILY PICKS UP THE SCENT

Wily was on the evening train to Venice. Albert had sent him a huge amount of information about Princess Parmigiano – documents, newspaper articles, audio files. She lived in the Palazzo Fandango on the main canal. She was an eighty-two-year-old antelope. She had been married to Prince Parmigiano until his death and since then she had married (and divorced) twice. The newspapers described her as "formidable" – in other words "completely terrifying".

Wily sat back in his seat and stared at the fields whizzing by. Somehow he had to persuade the princess to hand over the only bottle of Utopia in the world. But how?

An hour later the detective arrived in Venice and headed straight for the Palazzo Fandango. Light was shining from every window, animals were moving around inside and the sounds of music and conversation filled the air. Wily sprinted up the main steps and reached a set of huge double doors. He knocked loudly.

A butler wearing a white mask decorated with sequins and feathers opened the door. "Deliveries are round the back," he barked.

"I'm here to see the princess," said Wily.

"You can't be, you don't have a mask," said the butler. "This is a masked ball."

"I'm such a fool," Wily replied quickly, putting on a posh voice. "I thought it was a fancy-dress party. I don't suppose you have a spare mask, do you? I'm Baron Browntail – the princess's nephew's second cousin twice removed."

The butler sniffed. "Of course, sir. You should have said, sir." He beckoned Wily inside a large hallway and handed him a tiger mask.

Wily put on the mask and entered the gigantic ballroom. It was full of animals, most of them dancing, all of them wearing masks. How would he find Princess Parmigiano among this lot? He needed a plan – and fast. It had been almost four hours since the theft at Adolfo's launch. The villain could be gathering the ingredients to create Utopia right now.

An animal – probably a pony – in a clown mask waltzed by. Wily knew the princess was an antelope and that she was in her eighties. But there was no way for him to spot her among all the masked faces – he'd have to sniff out the princess instead.

Wily moved around the room, carefully picking up the different scents of the guests. He smelled seal and dog and even eagle.

After a couple of minutes, he caught his first scent of antelope. But this one was leaping and prancing – she was *not* eighty-something. His second antelope was male and his third was talking in a strong Russian accent. Finally, in a corner, he located an antelope resting on a walking stick. She was wearing – of all things – a fox mask.

Wily walked towards her. "Princess Parmigiano?" he said. "I'm here for your help."

"I don't know any Princess Parmigiano," drawled the voice behind the mask.

"Please," whispered Wily. "It's about Utopia. Thousands of animals' lives could be in danger."

Wily watched the eyes behind the mask blink slowly.

"Humph," she said. "Come with me."

Wily whipped off his mask and followed the princess out of the ballroom, along a corridor and up a winding staircase, taking in his surroundings for possible clues as they went. Soon they reached a large set of double steel doors. The princess removed her mask, tapped a number into a keypad and the doors slid open.

Wily found himself in a large pink room. There were shelves on every wall and bottles of perfume on every shelf. The doors of the room

slid shut. At the same time, Wily felt something move beside him. He spun round and saw that the princess had lifted up her cane and was aiming it at his head.

"Right, Signor Fox," she growled, "suppose you tell me what's *really* going on. There's a tranquillizer dart in my walking stick, so don't pull any stunts."

"OK, OK," said Wily, holding up his hands. He quickly explained why he was there.

The princess lowered her walking stick very slowly.

"Fine," she said, "but if you're a detective, prove it. Find the bottle of Utopia."

Wily looked at the princess and then at the endless shelves of perfume bottles. Wonderwhiff. Le Pong Parfait. Mega Scent. It would take him days to examine all these bottles. Then he had an idea. When the princess wasn't looking, Wily stamped the ground hard with his foot.

"Earthquake!" he gasped, as the perfume bottles tinkled.

"W-what?" stuttered the princess, glancing anxiously across the room.

Immediately, Wily ran over to an alcove. Sitting on a small shelf was a grubby bottle with no label. "Utopia!" he said with a smile.

"W-what? H-how?" stammered the princess.

"The moment you thought there was an earthquake, you looked over here, checking that your most precious bottle was safe," said Wily.

"Humph," said the princess coldly. "Well done."

"Now how about you give me what I came for?" asked Wily. "A sample of Utopia."

The princess shrugged. "OK, but hold your nose. Tightly."

Wily clamped his paw over his nose.

The princess placed a wad of cloth in each of her nostrils. Then she poured a tiny amount of Utopia into a plastic bottle.

Even though he was holding his nose tightly, Wily could detect a strange, sweet smell. He felt his eyes rolling backwards. He felt his stomach lurch. He was overwhelmed with feelings of joy.

"W-wow," he stammered.

"It doesn't take much," said the princess. "That's why it can never be used." She handed Wily the sample. "So guard this with your life."

Wily nodded.

"And perhaps when you've finished Adolfo's case, you can help me solve mine," she added.

"What do you mean?" asked Wily.

"I had an elegant young suitor," the princess said with a sigh. "He sent me flowers every day. Wrote me letters every week. And then two weeks ago, he vanished."

"Who was he?" asked Wily.

"I don't know – that's the problem," said the princess. "He always wore a mask. That's why I hold these masked balls, hoping he'll come back."

Wily started thinking. Could the princess's suitor and Adolfo's thief be the same person?

"Did he ever mention Utopia?" Wily asked.

The princess frowned. "Yes. He asked if it really existed. I said it was a secret, but that we'd have no secrets once we were married."

Wily was excited – this sounded suspicious. "Do you still have any of his letters?"

"Of course," said the princess. She took one out of her dress. "This is the first postcard he sent me."

Wily pulled out his magnifying glass and examined the handwriting. *To my beautiful Venetian angel.* That was fairly neutral, he thought. Then he looked at the postmark on the front: PISA.

PISA

PISA

5

To my beautiful
Venetian angel,
Love missed you

Princess Parmigiano,
Palazzo Fandango,
Main Canal
VENICE

Wily considered his main suspects. Rou Red Panda. Joey Weasel. Bianca Badger.

"While he wasn't looking, I took a lock of his hair, too," said the princess, handing the detective a tuft of hair from inside a locket.

Wily studied the lock of hair. It was black and white, like a badger's...

"And what was his voice like?" he asked.

"Hmm, quite soft and gentle, considering

he was male," said the princess. "But that may have been because he was talking through a mask. It muffles the voice, you see."

Wily nodded. All the clues pointed to Bianca. It looked like she had tried to get the bottle of Utopia by charming the princess. She'd disguised herself as a handsome stranger, but then the princess had said they'd have to get married and that was the end of that. Bianca had no choice but to steal the recipe from Adolfo instead.

Bianca worked for the *Pisan Gazette*. Why would she want the Utopia recipe?

Wily smiled and held up the perfume sample. "Thank you for this, Princess. I have what I need. Now I'll let you get back to your party."

A TRIP TO THE TOWER

Outside on the main canal, Wily hopped into a gondola.

"Train station, please," he said to the gondolier, a pelican in a straw hat. Then he called Albert on his smartphone.

The mole's face appeared on the screen.

"Albert, I've got the sample of Utopia. Can you send a messenger drone to meet me?"

"Of course," said Albert. "It'll be there in five minutes. Do you need any other gadgets?"

"Not yet," said Wily. "I'm trying to keep a low

36

profile – using trains and taxis … and gondolas."

"What's next?" asked Albert.

"Bianca Badger has become my main suspect," said Wily. "So I'm going to Pisa to find her."

"Why would a journalist want a perfume recipe?" asked Albert.

BIANCA

"I'm not sure yet," said Wily. "Maybe she wants to sell it to make money. Maybe she thinks it will generate news stories and she'll get all the exclusives."

At that moment, the pelican raised his voice. "Sorry to interrupt, Signor," he said, "but I think we're being followed."

Wily glanced over his shoulder and saw an animal in a hyena mask in the gondola behind.

"OK, Albert, gotta go," said Wily. "Send that drone as soon as you can."

"Shall I speed up?" asked the pelican.

"If you can," said Wily.

The pelican nodded and started to paddle twice as hard and twice as fast. The gondola behind them sped up, too.

Wily stared at the hyena mask and tried to puzzle out who was behind it. But the animal was wearing a black cloak covering their body.

"Is this as fast as you can go?" he asked.

The pelican nodded and puffed.

"OK, then get to the Grand Canal as quickly as you can," said Wily.

The pelican did as he was asked. But by the time they got there, the animal in the hyena mask was only a few metres behind them.

Wily looked around. There were gondolas on every side. He paid the pelican and then hopped on to another gondola.

"Sorry," said Wily to the animals in that gondola. Then he leaped on to another gondola and then another.

The hyena started to follow.

Wily glanced over his shoulder, grabbed a gondolier's oar then, using the oar like a pole vault, he flung himself across the water and landed in between two nanny goats in a speedboat. At the same time, he heard a buzzing noise overhead. Wily looked up and saw the drone that Albert had sent. It was a small black box with a propeller on top of it.

"How exciting," said one of the nanny goats. "Are you being chased by the police?"

"Something like that," said Wily, looking at the hyena, who was about to pole-vault across the water towards him.

"Leave it to us," said the nanny goat, shifting the boat into reverse. "And we'll save your friend, too." She started steering the speedboat towards the hyena.

"No! That's not my friend…" said Wily, as the hyena loomed closer.

Quick as a flash, the detective grabbed the drone. He took the Utopia sample out of his pocket and dropped it into the black box. Then, using the number panel on the side, he punched in the coordinates of Adolfo's mansion and pressed a large green button. The drone shot into the air just as the hyena landed on top of him.

At least I'll find out who the villain is, thought Wily, as he reached out and grabbed the mask. But there was nothing behind it. Instead Wily heard a loud splash. He looked into the canal and saw a dark streak in the water. With the sample of Utopia gone, the villain had decided to vanish, too.

Had it been Bianca Badger? Or someone working for her?

Wily turned to look at the nanny goats. "Can this thing get me to Pisa?" he asked.

Wily arrived in Pisa harbour the next morning. He thanked the nanny goats and headed straight for the offices of the *Pisan Gazette*.

"I need to speak to Bianca Badger," he said.

"I'm sorry," said the receptionist, "she's not in the office at the moment."

"Where is she, then?" said Wily.

The receptionist looked suspicious. "Who's asking?"

Wily quickly flashed a fake ID card at the receptionist. "I work for the Italian National Lottery. Miss Badger has won a sizeable prize. But so far she hasn't claimed it."

The receptionist gazed at Wily. "Really? How much are we talking?"

"I can only discuss this with Miss Badger. But it's OK – she still has sixty minutes left to claim it. Please tell her to call me at—"

"Oh, no," the receptionist interrupted. "I'll find her for you now. I can track her company phone using this clever gizmo on my desk."

She tapped a number into a panel. "So … she got back from Milan yesterday. And went straight to… *How strange.*"

"What's strange?" asked Wily.

"She spent the night at the Leaning Tower."

Five minutes later, Wily was staring at the Leaning Tower of Pisa. There were tourists milling around the bottom of the tower and some at the top, enjoying the view.

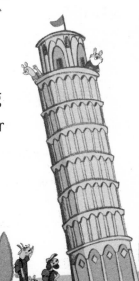

The detective breathed in, trying to pick up on the scent of badger, but there were too many other smells in the air.

What was Bianca doing here? If this was her hideout, it was a strange place to choose.

Wily bought a ticket and climbed up the tower. He looked in every room and sniffed along the colonnades. No Bianca. Maybe this was a false trail. But as he walked back down the staircase, a thought struck him: *Why is the tower leaning?* Something *underground* must be causing it.

Back outside, Wily looked around carefully. Then he saw it – a patch of grass that was a different shade from the rest. He took out his magnifying glass and examined the patch more closely. It was a flap of *fake* grass!

Wily made sure no one was looking, then slowly lifted up the flap. Underneath there was a hole. A badger hole? There was only one way to find out.

He dived in and found himself tumbling head over heels down a dirt chute. He landed with a thump on a heap of boxes and pots.

Feeling slightly dazed, Wily stood up. He was in a large underground burrow and he seemed to be alone. He looked at the objects he had collided with.

Two tubs of black sticky stuff.

A metal box marked "Perfume recipes".

A wooden crate full of maps.

A small safe with a timer taped to the top.

Wily started by opening the metal box, but it was empty. He looked inside the wooden crate and saw maps of Venice and Milan covered with red dots. He also found a detailed drawing of the streets around Adolfo's house and a floorplan of Adolfo's mansion with a cross in his bedroom.

So this *was* the villain's hideout. But was Bianca the villain? He breathed in – there were lots of different scents, and one of them was definitely badger.

So where was she?

Wily picked up one of the tubs of black stuff and thought about what it might be. One was empty. One was half empty. He looked around, but there was no sign of the black stuff covering anything in the burrow.

Finally, Wily glanced at the safe. There were wires coming out of the back. He guessed that if anyone tried to open it, some kind of bomb would go off. Albert would know how to deal with it.

Wily was just getting out his phone when he heard a deep snarling voice behind him.

"Hold it right there, Wily Fox."

JULIUS BLOWS IT

Wily turned round slowly. His shoulders were tense, his teeth were clenched. Then he saw who it was and relaxed.

It was Detective Julius Hound from PSSST – the Police Spy, Sleuth and Snoop Taskforce. Next to him was Sergeant Sybil Squirrel.

Julius and Wily always seemed to end up investigating the same case. And Julius didn't like it one bit.

"What are you doing here?" barked Julius.

"What are *you* doing here?" replied Wily.

"Official police business," said Julius. "Top secret."

"Important client business," said Wily. "Very hush-hush."

"Honestly, you two," said Sybil Squirrel, "the cases must be connected. Otherwise, why would we all end up in a burrow underneath the Leaning Tower of Pisa?"

Wily grunted. Julius snarled.

"Can't you put your egos to one side and work together for a change?" said Sybil.

Wily huffed and then said, "OK, Sybil, if you must know, I'm looking into the theft of a perfume recipe."

Julius burst out laughing. "That sounds serious. What else has gone missing? Priceless shampoo? Precious lemon-scented wipes?"

Wily blinked, refusing to react.

"Well, *we* are investigating an attempted bank robbery," said Julius. "We followed the suspects' scent here. Three crafty scoundrels, known as the Black Paw Gang. Let's have a look at what they've left behind." He picked up one of the tubs of black stuff.

"I've been through everything already," said Wily. "They're linked to my case, not yours. A plan of Adolfo Aroma's house, an empty box marked 'Perfume recipes'."

"I'll be the judge of that," said Julius, sniffing around the safe. "And we need to bust this thing open. It could have vital evidence inside."

"OK, but it's clearly rigged to explode," said Wily. "Let me call Albert – he knows how to defuse bombs."

"I don't need the help of a silly mole," growled Julius. He jerked one of the wires coming out of the timer. It gave a loud beep and started counting down from ten.

Wily sighed. "That's blown it. Come on, Sybil, let's get out of here."

"It's probably just a bluff," said Julius. But Wily and Sybil were already scampering back up the chute.

They got out just in time. There was a muffled boom from under the Leaning Tower. Julius flew out of the burrow like a cannonball, landing with a *whoompf* in a nearby tree.

At the same time, the Leaning Tower lurched to the right ... and came to a stop – standing straight up.

"Looks like the Leaning Tower of Pisa is now just the Tower of Pisa," said Wily.

A moaning sound came from the shops and tourist stalls around the tower. Shopkeepers were staring up at the now-vertical tower. Some of them were tearing up their postcards and others were flinging their souvenir T-shirts to the ground.

One of them was wailing, "I'm ruined!"

"Time I left," said Wily. "Good luck, Sybil."

The detective disappeared into a crowd of tourists and headed down an alleyway. He had to work out where to go next. Bianca – if she was the villain – hadn't been in her hideout. And now the evidence was gone.

A moment later, his phone started to buzz. It was a video call from Adolfo. "Everything OK, Mr Fox?" the perfume maker asked.

"Having a blast," replied Wily. "Did you get the Utopia sample?"

"Yes," said Adolfo. "I've analyzed the ingredients and you're right – it contains something very special, which could lead us to the thief."

"What's that?" asked Wily.

"Hai lee niffi. It's a rare purple flower that only grows on the highest slopes of Jade Dragon Snow Mountain in China," said Adolfo.

"Sounds like that's where I'm heading next, then," said Wily. "And has Paulo found any more clues?"

"Ah, he's no longer with us, I'm afraid," said Adolfo. "Said he'd let me down ... that he wasn't cut out for a job in crime prevention, after all."

Wily thought for a moment. "Maybe he was a bit careless, but I didn't think he'd give up so easily. Have you found a replacement? You need to protect that Utopia sample."

"Don't worry, Mr Fox," said Adolfo, "I've got rid of the perfume already. And I'll advise Princess Parmigiano to do the same."

Wily hung up and immediately put in a video call to Albert. The detective hadn't been to China in years – not since the Case of the Seven Stuffed Pandas – and he was going to need some help.

When Albert's face appeared on screen, Wily told him the latest developments.

"The hai lee niffi flower?" said Albert. "Never heard of it. And there's nothing about it online. But for Jade Dragon Snow Mountain, you'll need to fly to Chengdu. I'll make sure there are tickets and a fake passport waiting for you at Pisa airport."

"Thanks, Albert," said Wily.

"I've got a few new gadgets that might help you, too," Albert added, his tiny eyes twinkling, "but it's probably best to show you those in person. I'll meet you in Chengdu. And there's something else."

"What?"

"Why do you have black stuff all over your face?" said Albert.

Wily rubbed his cheek with his paw. "Oh, it's from the explosion."

He looked at the goo on his paw.

"Hang on, it's face paint," he murmured. "The stuff actors use. Designed to stick to fur. Why would the villain need face paint?"

Perhaps he would find the answer in China.

THE ONLY WAY IS UP

During the flight, Wily went over the facts
of the case. Bianca Badger appeared to be
the obvious suspect – her quick exit from
Milan, her mobile phone signal at the Leaning
Tower, the scent of badger in the underground
hideout. But … but … what was the black face
paint for? And why hadn't Bianca been in her
hideout? Was there something obvious that he
hadn't seen yet?

"Earplugs, sir?" said a high-pitched voice
above him.

"Excuse me?"

"Earplugs?" It was the flight attendant, a tall stork with bright purple lipstick. "They stop your ears popping during the flight."

Wily took the earplugs and looked at them. They were long tubes of yellow sponge. He put them in his ears and blinked. Extraordinary. He couldn't hear a thing.

He was about to drift off to sleep when he noticed something else. With his eyes shut and his ears blocked, he was suddenly aware of all the smells on the plane. And he smelled something that made him jump.

Adolfo.

No. Not Adolfo. Something or someone who had been at Adolfo's launch party.

He opened his eyes and stood up in his seat.

He glanced at the animals on the flight. He saw shrews, a mongoose, six pandas, two sheep and an assortment of other animals, but nobody he recognized. He sat back down again and tried to pick up the scent once more. It was gone.

When they landed in Chengdu, Wily lingered by the baggage reclaim area, watching as the animals from his flight came through, trying to work out if any of the faces were familiar. There were the shrews, the pandas, the mongoose again, but no Bianca Badger, no Rou Red Panda and no Joey Weasel. What wasn't he seeing?

The detective walked through the arrivals gate. A split second later, he felt someone tapping him on the shoulder. Wily turned round and there was Albert.

"How did you get here faster than me?" he asked.

Albert rolled up his trouser leg. "Telekinetic Booster Boots. They might be ready for your next case. But right now I've brought you some other gadgets."

Wily followed the mole outside and down a side street, where a black rickshaw was parked.

"It drives itself," Albert explained. He pointed to a microphone. "Speak your destination into there. Clap once to go, and twice to stop."

"Brilliant," said Wily, climbing inside. "And how do I make it go really, really fast?"

Albert sighed. "Clap four times," he said.

"Excellent," said Wily and held up his hands, preparing to clap.

"Wait – your disguise," said Albert. "Whoever stole the recipe is clearly ruthless. They could have killed you in Venice."

He gave Wily a rucksack containing a bright red baggy outfit and a large metal baton.

"You are Wang," said Albert, "the Shanghai Scorcher, a fire-eater in the Chinese State Circus." He held up the metal baton and breathed on it. A huge plume of fire shot out of the end. "Press this button when you put it in your mouth, and the fire will go out," he explained.

"Nice one, Albert," said Wily. "I'll practise later. But right now, there's no time to lose. I've got to find where the hai lee niffi flower grows. That's where our criminal will be."

"OK," said Albert, "I'll be on our usual secure line. Report to me every hour."

Wily nodded and said into the microphone, "Jade Dragon Snow Mountain."

The rickshaw whirred into life. Wily clapped four times and it shot off like a bullet, leaving Albert sighing and shaking his head.

Wily soon left the city behind. Wooden houses and paddy fields whizzed by. It was not long before he was starting to climb Jade Dragon Snow Mountain.

Everything was covered in snow. The trees, the rocks, the path – all of it was crisp and white. The rickshaw started to slow down as the snow got deeper and the path got steeper.

"Come on," Wily muttered. But the rickshaw grew slower and slower.

Wily glanced up the mountain. The upper slopes were still a long way off, surrounded by a halo of clouds.

The rickshaw gave one last lurch forward and then ground to a halt.

Wily groaned. He was going to have to climb the rest of the way. But then he had a thought. Albert often put extra features into his inventions. Things he was testing out. Things he didn't tell Wily about.

Wily clicked his fingers. He whistled. He tried clapping four times again.

Nothing happened.

He tried clapping five times, then six.

That was it!

The two long poles at the side of the rickshaw slid forward, flipped over and buried themselves in the snow.

They looked like … stilts.

Wily leaped out of the rickshaw and grabbed his disguise. Then he planted his feet on the stilts.

Wily lifted his right foot up slightly and the stilt sprang out of the snow, swung itself forward and planted itself back down further up the mountain.

Then he did the same with his left foot.

These weren't just stilts – they were steam-powered, spring-loaded cybernetic stilts.

Wily strode up the mountain, planting the stilts in the snow, covering a hundred metres a minute. He knew that the flowers grew on "the highest slopes", but Wily was nearly at the top of the mountain – he couldn't get much higher – and still there was no sign of them anywhere.

Wily lifted his right foot for a final push to the top, but it was too steep even for the stilts. The poles tilted forward, hurling Wily into a snow-covered juniper bush.

The detective clambered to his feet and stuck his head out of the bush. He couldn't believe his eyes. Behind the bush was a small field without any snow on it. And it was full of purple flowers. Wily breathed in. The air smelled beautiful.

These must *be the hai lee niffi flowers!* Wily thought.

He immediately checked to see if any had been picked. No. All the stalks had flowers, there were no holes in the soil. He looked for footprints in the snow surrounding the field. There were none. Excellent – he was in time. Now all he had to do was hide there and wait for the thief to arrive.

Wily went back to the juniper bush. He positioned his phone on a branch, set it to video mode and programmed it to beep loudly if it picked up a heat signature from any other animal. Then he called Albert. Albert's face immediately appeared on the screen.

"Wily! How can you be there already? It's taken you less than an hour... Hang on, are those my stilts buried in the snow?"

"Er..."

"But they weren't finished!"

"You're missing the point, Albert," said Wily. "Thanks to you, I've overtaken the thief. I'm lying in wait for them now."

"But the rickshaw will be in pieces. How are you going to get back down?" said Albert.

"I'll think of something," said Wily. "But right now I'm sending you some photos of the flowers. I need you to find out more about them – how they grow, what plant family they're in… Anything you can."

"OK," said Albert grumpily. "I'll try again."

Wily hung up and then he watched and he waited. An hour passed.

He watched some more. Another hour passed.

He must have dozed off because suddenly the sound of his phone gave him a start.

"Wily, it's me." Albert's face appeared. "From the petals and the stalk thickness, I believe your mystery flowers belong to the compositae family."

"OK," said Wily, trying to look like he'd been awake the whole time.

"They're like blue daisies, but with deeper roots. Maybe that's why they produce such amazing perfume. Their roots draw all kinds of minerals out of the soil."

"Maybe," said Wily. Then he looked at the field and gasped. At least twenty flowers had gone.

Wily raced across to where the flowers had been. His phone hadn't beeped – no animal had been near the flowers. There were no footprints in the snow – so what had happened?

"Albert," said Wily, "I don't know how but…"

At that moment, a flower on the other side of the field started to tremble. It shook for a couple of seconds and then vanished underground.

"It's the roots!" Wily exclaimed.

He spotted another flower trembling. He hung up on Albert, raced across the field and grabbed the flower. Someone underground was tugging the roots. Wily tugged the stalk hard. The animal pulled the roots even harder. The flower started to stretch but it didn't snap. Eventually the animal gave up and another flower started to twitch.

This time Wily let the animal take the flower. But as the flower disappeared, he held the stalk gently and allowed his arm to be pulled underground. Then he tried to grab the animal with his hand. He felt fur – and then a foot – and then a nasty bite.

"Ow!" Wily yanked his arm out of the hole and started to burrow. Within five seconds, he reached a network of tunnels that had been dug underneath the field. He saw a flash of dust and gave chase. The tunnels were slightly too narrow for his body, so he had to keep stopping to move clods of earth and pebbles out of the way.

Wily reached a crossroads. He listened. He heard a scurrying from one of the tunnels, then a squeak from the other. He decided to follow the squeak. He ran faster and the squeak got louder. He was catching up.

The tunnel curved and Wily increased his speed. Then he bumped into an elderly mouse. The mouse fell on his back and gave an ear-splitting EEK!

"Sorry," stammered Wily, "but I don't suppose you saw a badger passing this way."

"This is China, young man," said the mouse, "we don't get any badgers. It's mostly red pandas up here."

"Red pandas," Wily said. "Did a red panda dig this tunnel?"

But the mouse had already tottered off.

Wily looked down at his front paw. Earlier, he'd grabbed the thief's tail. Now he was holding a clump of fluffy white fur. A badger's tail wasn't that white or that fluffy. But a red panda's tail was...

Rou Red Panda. She owned the biggest department store in Beijing. Was she planning to make her own perfume? And then sell it – illegally – on the black market?

Wily thought about the black face paint he'd found in Pisa. If Rou had painted her fur black, she'd look a bit like a ... badger.

Could *she* have been Princess Parmigiano's secret admirer?

Had she also been the animal in the hyena mask?

Wily looked again at the fur in his hand. He smelled it. All he could detect was the hai lee niffi flower. It drowned out all other smells and scents.

He needed to find Rou Red Panda. If she was the thief, she was one step closer to making Utopia.

She had at least twenty hai lee niffi flowers.

She had the secret ingredient.

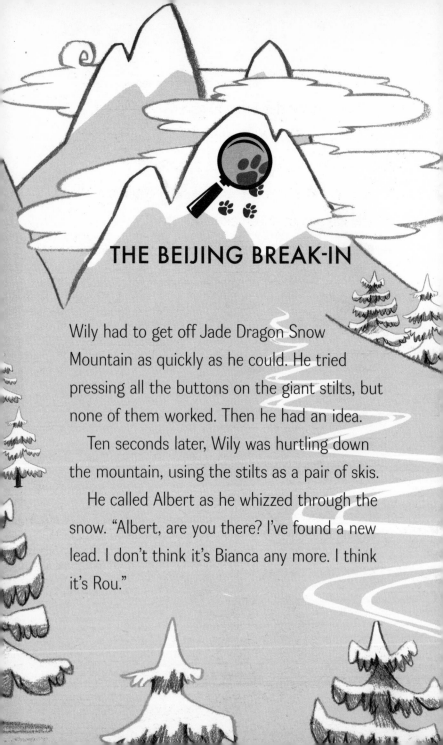

THE BEIJING BREAK-IN

Wily had to get off Jade Dragon Snow Mountain as quickly as he could. He tried pressing all the buttons on the giant stilts, but none of them worked. Then he had an idea.

Ten seconds later, Wily was hurtling down the mountain, using the stilts as a pair of skis.

He called Albert as he whizzed through the snow. "Albert, are you there? I've found a new lead. I don't think it's Bianca any more. I think it's Rou."

"Rou Red Panda? Are you sure?" said Albert.

"Think about it. She owns a huge department store in Beijing. She has lots of wealthy customers. If she made Utopia, she could sell the bottles in secret and make a fortune."

A tree branch whipped towards Wily. He ducked and kept skiing.

"But why would she have a hideout in Pisa?" asked Albert.

"That was her base in Italy," said Wily. "While she was trying to get the recipe."

"I see," said Albert. "OK, I'll meet you in Beijing. The quickest way for you to get there is on the bullet train. There's one passing Luhuzho in fifteen minutes – it's right at the bottom of the mountain."

"Thanks, Albert." Wily hung up and whooshed off down to Luhuzho.

As he approached the bottom of the mountain, he could see the railway tracks curving round the hillside and into a tunnel. And there was the bullet train, flying along at an astonishing speed. He was going to miss it!

Wily skied faster. When he reached the railway line he flung himself towards the train, but too late – it was gone. Wily landed on the tracks, one ski on each rail. Sparks flew off the back of them as he whizzed along. He could see the train ahead, but it was disappearing fast.

Could he catch up?

Further up the track, Wily saw a railway tunnel and, in front of the tunnel, there was a signal box showing a green light. He pulled off his left ski and threw it like a javelin, hitting the signal box and turning the light red.

The bullet train screeched to a halt, Wily unhitched himself from the other ski and did a forward roll on to the back ledge of the train. Then he threw the ski at the signal box and turned the light back to green.

"Faster than a speeding bullet," he said with a smile.

The train arrived in Beijing two hours later. Wily had spent the journey reading about Rou and her business empire. Her flagship store was in Wangfujing, not far from Beijing's central train station.

He'd need to watch the place closely – without being seen. He wondered if he'd need to go via a clothes shop, to pick up a disguise. But then he remembered – Albert had already put the perfect thing in his rucksack.

When Wily walked out of the train station, he was the circus performer Wang, the Shanghai Scorcher, wearing a red baggy jumpsuit and holding a metal baton.

It wasn't long before Wily was standing outside the department store, along with the tourists, street performers and market traders. He secretly took pictures as he waited.

Just ten minutes later, Wily saw Rou walking towards the store. She must have flown back from Chengdu and arrived just after him. She walked past the entrance and down the street that ran along the side of her store.

Wily followed. She went into a blue door marked "RRP Laboratories". There was a security camera just above it and a keypad beneath the door handle.

Wily needed to think fast. Rou had the hai lee niffi flowers. She had the recipe. She was going to work in her laboratory right now. Wily swore that he could smell perfume – a beautiful perfume – the most beautiful smell he had ever smelled…

He pulled out his metal torch and breathed fire on the security camera, melting it instantly. Then he breathed fire on the keypad, turning it into a blob of molten metal, and pushed open the door. It would probably trigger an alarm, but he'd get a minute, maybe more, to explore.

Wily ran down a long white corridor. He turned a corner and saw a bare laboratory with a workbench covered in empty vials and test tubes. He kept on running until he reached a door at the end of another long corridor. A sign above it read:

NEW PERFUME UNIT

This must be it.

Wily opened the door. There was nobody there. But the room was full of Bunsen burners and metal stands holding wiggly plastic tubes full of bubbling liquid. He glanced around, looking for the purple flowers. He breathed in, trying to smell them. Instead all he could detect was red panda. Which was not surprising because, at that moment, Rou was flying through the air towards him. With a deafening "Hiii-ya!" she booted Wily in the side with her outstretched leg.

Wily landed on his bottom with a crunch.

"Got you!" she exclaimed. "Now don't move – I am a master at kung-fu." Wily tried to get up, but Rou whacked him on the head with the side of her hand. "I said, don't move," she continued. "The police will be here any second."

"The p-police?" stammered Wily. "You've called the police?"

"Of course I have," said Rou. "You're going to prison. You stole my best equipment this morning and now you're back for the rest."

"Hang on," said Wily. "*I've* done nothing. *You* took Adolfo's recipe. *You* picked the hai lee niffi flowers from Jade Dragon Snow Mountain."

Rou looked genuinely stunned. "I didn't take Adolfo's recipe or the flowers," she said. "Oh good, here are the police."

Wily turned round and there in the doorway stood Julius Hound and Sybil Squirrel.

THE GREAT ESCAPE

"Wily Fox," growled Julius. "Just as I thought."

"Julius!" exclaimed Wily. "What are *you* doing in China? Last time we met, you'd just blown up the Leaning Tower of Pisa."

"That had NOTHING to do with me," Julius huffed, going red. "Besides, *I'm* the one asking questions here. Why have you broken into this young panda's laboratory?"

"Because of the case I'm investigating. The perfume one I told you about," said Wily.

"Well, we're in China because of the case

we're investigating. The one where banks get robbed. And I think you can tell us something about that, too," said Julius.

"Look," said Rou, "are you going to arrest him, or not? Because somebody stole my equipment this morning. And he looks pretty guilty to me."

"He certainly does," said Julius. "You're up to your eyeballs in it, Fox. Here we are in China, investigating our best lead yet in the Black Paw Gang case, and – guess what – we intercept a text message from the gang leader that mentions you. Then five minutes later we hear on the police radio that a fox has been caught breaking into a perfume lab. And – what a coincidence – it's you."

"Hang on – a text message? What are you talking about?" said Wily.

"Show him, Sybil," barked Julius.

Sybil Squirrel handed Wily a slip of paper.

MEET RHONDA WALLABY INSIDE LIBRARY. YODELLING FORBIDDEN ON XYLOPHONE. CITY AARDVARK NOSES HAVE ESPECIALLY LUMPY PERFUME.

"But this is gibberish," said Wily.

"That's what I thought," said Julius. "Until I deciphered the code."

Sybil cleared her throat loudly.

"OK, Sybil might have helped me a bit," growled Julius. "Read the first initials."

Wily went back to the message and read the first letter of each word:

MR WILY FOX CAN HELP

Wily blinked. "But ... but..."

"Sorry, old friend, it does look a bit suspicious," said Sybil, clipping a pair of handcuffs round Wily's wrists.

"You're coming with us to Beijing Central Police Station and you're going to tell us everything you know," snarled Julius, hustling Wily out of the room. He raised his hat to Rou. "Thank you for helping us to catch this notorious criminal."

Julius pushed Wily out into the alley and bundled him into the back of a police van. Sybil got inside with him and then Julius drove off.

Wily sat thinking, not saying anything. Then something wafted up his nose.

"What's that horrible smell?" he whispered.

"Do you mean this?" Sybil pulled a phone out of her pocket. "It was left behind at the last bank robbery we investigated. It smells way better than it used to."

Wily sniffed and sniffed. It was foul, revolting, loathsome – he felt like passing out. Where had he smelled it before?

Then everything clicked into place. It made sense all of a sudden!

It was the same smell that had nearly knocked him out at the Smellissimo launch – when the bottles had been switched. When the Utopia recipe had been stolen.

"Sybil, our cases ... are the *same* case..." Wily mumbled.

"I told you that in Pisa," said Sybil.

"Yes, but I think I've cracked it," said Wily. "I can't believe I didn't see it before. Or *smell* it before."

"What do you mean?"

"That horrible stinky liquid they put in the Smellissimo bottle. I got rotten eggs and cowpats and ... and ... this." Wily held up the smelly phone. "Skunk," he said.

"Skunk?" said Sybil, and then her eyes lit up. "Skunk!"

"Hand me your notepad," said Wily. "This is your criminal."

Wily took Sybil's notepad and drew a sketch. Then he showed it to Sybil. It was Paulo Polecat.

"But that's not a skunk," said Sybil.

Wily used the rubber to make a thin white line on Paulo's back.

"Now it is," said Wily.

"OK, but what has all this got to do with perfume?" asked Sybil.

Wily briefly explained what had happened at the Smellissimo launch.

"Paulo was Adolfo's head of security," said Wily. "He's the only one who could have switched the bottles. He used his own nasty skunk scent to make a horrible concoction. Then he mixed in other stinky smells to cover it up."

"OK, but how did he steal the Utopia recipe?" Sybil replied.

"Easy," said Wily, "he must have been told the combination of the safe. In his haste he got it wrong, which is why he left teeth marks on the edge of the safe – he was frustrated. But once he'd got the recipe, getting away was easy."

"Why?"

"Because he was the only animal in the whole building who wasn't searched. I can't believe he fooled me. He painted his white stripe out with black face paint! I should have suspected something when he resigned the day after the recipe went missing."

The van hit a bump and Sybil said, "We'll be at the police station in a few minutes. What do you want to do?"

"What do you think?" said Wily. "You've got to get me out of here."

"You know I can't do that," said Sybil. "Besides, you've told me how this Paulo Skunk guy is involved in your case. But how's he involved with mine?"

"I don't know yet," said Wily, "but that phone you found is covered with his scent. He was in that bank."

Sybil didn't say anything. She was thinking.

"This is serious, Sybil," said Wily. "I'm certain he stole those hai lee niffi flowers. And it must have been him that broke into Rou Red Panda's lab this morning. To steal all the equipment he needs to make Utopia. But why does he need to make it here? What's he got planned?

We've got to find him."

Sybil thought for a few more seconds. Then she undid Wily's handcuffs and opened the back of the van.

"I'm doing this on one condition," she said. "That you take me with you."

"Deal," said Wily with a smile.

And out they jumped.

WILY CRACKS THE CODE

Sybil and Wily tumbled out of the police van and came to rest by a lamp post. They stood up and brushed themselves down. At that moment, a manhole cover by their feet lifted up and a mole's head popped out.

"Albert!" said Wily. "How did you know where I was?"

"There's a tracker in your phone," said Albert. "I've been listening to police radio. Apparently you've been arrested. Again."

"That's her fault," said Wily, grinning at Sybil.

They jumped down through the manhole
and landed in a wide sewage pipe. Albert had
set up base at the end of a narrow tunnel. It
contained a laptop, a workbench and a range of
small gadgets covered in buttons and blinking
lights. There were two upside-down milk crates
on the floor.

Wily sat down on one of them and quickly
explained his new theory to Albert.

"We need to go through the evidence
again," he said. "Work out where Paulo might
be and why."

"Where shall we start?" asked Sybil.

"Maybe with the perfume. If they've started making it, you'd expect to see police reports of people collapsing or falling into a trance. And then check the air-quality office. They might see traces of unexpected gases and smells."

Albert started typing away at the computer. He held one headphone up to his ear.

"Nothing on any of the police frequencies – except about you two escaping," he said.

At that moment, there was a strange bang in a distant tunnel.

"Ignore that," said Albert. "It's just maintenance work. Been happening since I got here."

Then he typed something else into the computer.

"Checking the Beijing air-quality statistics. Nothing unusual so far," he reported.

"Let's think about my case, then," said Sybil, "and how the perfume might be linked to the bank robberies."

"Good idea," said Wily. "Albert, can you hack into every bank security camera in Beijing? Check for anything odd."

"Piece of cake," said Albert. He brought up one grainy security picture after another, clicking through them at lightning speed.

"Nothing … no … nope … not a thing … no."

"OK, so they've not stolen anything yet," said Wily. "Sybil, can you tell us anything about their methods?"

There was another bang in the distance.

"Sure," said Sybil. "But this is the weird bit – they've broken into about five banks, and so far they haven't stolen much."

"What?" said Wily and Albert together.

"Yeah, it's strange," said Sybil. "They're great

at shutting down the alarms and getting into the safe. But then they take maybe one bag of cash or nothing at all. They leave a really strong scent, though. That's why we've been able to track them."

Another bang sounded in a distant tunnel – even louder this time.

"They sound like terrible bank robbers," said Albert.

But Wily was listening to the echo of the explosion.

"What is this maintenance work?" he asked.

"Something over at the Forbidden City," said Albert. "That's where it's coming from."

Wily looked thoughtful. "Forbidden City … Forbidden City…" he murmured.

"Yes," said Albert, "it's the most famous place in Beijing. A huge walled palace where the Emperors used to live and—"

"I know what the Forbidden City is," said Wily. "Sybil, can you let me see that message again? The one from the bad guys. Albert, check to see if there's any planned maintenance work going on in the sewers of Beijing today."

Sybil handed Wily the slip of paper.

MEET RHONDA WALLABY INSIDE LIBRARY. YODELLING FORBIDDEN ON XYLOPHONE. CITY AARDVARK NOSES HAVE ESPECIALLY LUMPY PERFUME.

Wily looked at the words FORBIDDEN and CITY and then started muttering again.

"What is it, Wily?" asked Sybil.

"It's code all right," said Wily, "but it's got nothing to do with the first initials. Paulo must have done that to try and set me up. Read every third word."

Sybil read: MEET INSIDE FORBIDDEN CITY HAVE PERFUME

At the same time, Albert said, "There's nothing planned. It can't be maintenance work, after all."

"Someone's blowing things up underneath the Forbidden City," said Wily. "And I bet it's Paulo. What's the quickest way there, Albert?"

"Well, it would be on my old rocket-powered Vespa, but you broke that," said Albert.

"OK, the second quickest, then."

"The self-driving rickshaw, but—"

"I know, I broke that, too. What's the third?"

"Running," said Albert. "Really fast."

"Humph," said Wily. "OK, which way?"

Sybil and Wily followed Albert as he trotted through the sewers, turning down side tunnels, scurrying into dark hatches.

After a few minutes, Wily's nostrils were hit by a wave of strong perfume. He blinked and for a second his eyes went misty.

"We're on the right track," said Wily, "I just got a whiff of Utopia. Be careful – if the scent gets too strong, we'll have to turn back."

But the smell soon passed away.

There was another explosion and the walls of the sewer pipe shook.

"What do you think they're doing?" asked Sybil.

"They must be breaking into the palace," said Wily. "Maybe they got fed up with banks. But I can't work out how it links to Utopia."

"Can't anyone else hear the noise they're making? Isn't there any security at the Forbidden City?" asked Sybil.

They turned a corner of the sewer and saw a row of guards slumped against the tunnel wall.

They were all staring into space, with smiles on their faces. There was a faint smell of Utopia in the air.

Albert leaned over and peered into their eyes.

"They're still alive but..."

"In a trance," said Wily. "And I guess we've got our answer – that's what Utopia is for. Knocking out anyone who gets in their way."

They walked on and found themselves in a large underground cavern. Above, there was a hole and light was streaming in.

"This must be the sewer underneath the Forbidden City," whispered Albert.

"And that must be the hole they made with all those explosions," Sybil whispered back.

At that moment, something was lowered through the hole. Wily, Sybil and Albert hid behind the nearest object they could find – a workbench covered with test tubes and bottles of liquid. It tinkled slightly as they scrambled behind it, but then everything was silent.

Wily and Sybil peered out.

A guard was being lowered through the hole in the roof. He had a rope tied firmly round his waist and he was smiling. His body hit the bottom of the cavern and then he slumped to one side.

A skunk shimmied down the rope after the guard. He whistled, and a second skunk slid down.

"Boss! Boss!" the first skunk called out.

At the far end of the cavern, a shape emerged from the shadows. Wily recognized his outline immediately. It was Paulo Polecat.

"OK, that was the last guard, boss," the skunk said.

"You're sure?" asked Paulo.

"Yeah, the Forbidden City closed to the public half an hour ago. They put on five evening guards. Four are in the tunnel back there. This is the last one."

"Good," said Paulo. "Now grab the swag bags and the tools. Let's get back up there and start looting."

Albert looked at Wily.

Wily held up his hand and mouthed, "Stay right here."

A split second later, Sybil's police radio came to life with a loud crackle:

Sybil Squirrel, are you receiving me? Sybil Squirrel?

It was Julius's barking voice.

Wily put his head in his hands.

Sybil tried to find her radio, desperate to switch it off, but instead she bumped into the workbench. A test tube rolled on to the ground, shattering into hundreds of pieces.

Julius's voice was still crackling:

Has that Fox kidnapped you? Where are you?

But now Paulo and the other two skunks were standing over them.

"Hello, Wily Fox," growled Paulo. "Been playing with Rou's chemistry set?"

His voice was rougher and meaner now.

"Hello, Paulo," said Wily, standing up slowly.

"Nah," said Paulo, "it's Duncan Skunk. Paulo's just a name I made up."

The two other skunks started to snigger.

"Are you a clown in a circus or something?" asked the first skunk.

Wily glanced down at his fire-eater's outfit. "You're the only clown round here, pal," he replied.

The skunk snarled and lurched forward, but Paulo – or Duncan – held him back.

"Easy," said Duncan. "Wily Fox, please meet my brother Sam and my cousin Simon."

"Otherwise known as the Black Paw Gang," said Wily.

Duncan Skunk's eyes narrowed. "Not bad, Fox. What else do you know?"

"That you've been trying to get your dirty paws on Utopia for months," said Wily. "First, you disguised yourself as a mysterious stranger and tried to persuade Princess Parmigiano to give you her bottle. Then, she insisted on getting married."

"Actually, she wanted a two-year engagement," Duncan said. "I couldn't wait that long."

"So you targeted Adolfo instead," Wily continued. "You knew Adolfo's father had made the perfume and that the recipe was locked in a high-security safe in the Aroma mansion. So you disguised yourself as a polecat, painting out your white stripe with black face paint, and pretended to be a security expert.

"On the launch night of Smellissimo, you switched the bottles and when everyone was passing out, you stole the recipe. You hung around afterwards to avoid suspicion, but as soon as I'd left, you resigned, pretending to be ashamed of yourself."

"Which you should be," huffed Sybil, shaking her tiny fist at Duncan.

"You knew I was going to Venice," Wily continued. "You were the only person I told except Albert and Adolfo – so you followed me there."

"Uh-uh," said Duncan, waving his finger. "I was still at Adolfo's, remember. Couldn't be in two places at once."

"That was me behind the hyena mask," said Simon. "Duncan warned me you were coming."

"I guess you tried to hack my phone, too," said Wily.

Duncan nodded. "It worked for a couple of minutes. Until your pint-sized pal cottoned on." He nodded at Albert. "Then I had to be *friendly* to you to get the information I needed. Fortunately you fell for my nice-guy act."

"What about Bianca Badger? Did she fall for it, too?" asked Wily.

"So you worked that out, eh?" Paulo said.

"Sort of," said Wily. "I know she was at the Leaning Tower."

"Yeah," growled Simon, "trying to *blackmail* us."

"She'd discovered something fishy was going on under the Leaning Tower," said Duncan, "but she didn't know what. We told her. Then we knocked her out with our stinky spray, tied her up and put her on a slow boat to Rio de Janeiro. She should be there by now."

"Well, it threw me off the scent," said Wily. "For a day or two. But I picked it up again. And I've caught you now."

"I don't think so, Fox," said Duncan, and he held up a bottle of purple liquid. "Welcome to Utopia."

"You're going to have a nice sleep," said Sam.

"Then we're going to nick every jewel in the Forbidden City," said Simon.

"And nobody will ever know we were there," said Duncan.

"Ah, I see. NOW I get it," said Wily.

"What do you get?" Duncan sneered.

"I thought you needed Utopia to knock everyone out," said Wily, "but you can do that already with your stinky scent – just like you did to Bianca. You need Utopia to cover your tracks."

"Not bad, Fox," hissed Duncan. "Do go on."

"You're awful. You're rubbish," said Wily. "You're the worst bank robbers in history. Sybil told me how you never managed to steal anything. Now I understand. When a skunk sprays, you can smell it miles away. Only the most beautiful smell in the world could hide a skunk's stupefying scent."

"I still don't get it," said Albert.

"Whiskers has cracked it," said Duncan with a grin. "Shame you'll be drooling like an idiot for the next two weeks. Yeah, we ain't had much luck with the bank robbery lark. What happens is, we break in – fine. We crack the safe – fine. Then one of us gets nervous."

"Usually you," said Sam to Simon.

"Usually *you*," said Simon to Sam.

"And we'll spray," said Duncan. "Everywhere. Then we have to split. There's no point in stealing anything and hoping to get away with it. Best chance we've got is to hop it. That way, it won't look serious and they won't put their best animals on it."

"Charming," said Sybil.

"Of course, now we've got Utopia," Duncan went on, "we can spray when we like, where we like. Utopia masks everything. We could be ten times as stinky and you'd still never pick up our whiff. Nose pegs on, boys," he said.

Duncan put a long black clothes peg on his nose. Sam and Simon did the same. Then Duncan opened the bottle of Utopia.

"You might have noticed," he said. "Utopia has this side benefit, too. As well as masking any smell we make, it also knocks everyone out – for much longer than our spray ever could."

Wily could sense the beautiful smell tingling his nostrils.

"Sweet dreams," said Duncan.

Albert hit the floor with a bump. He was grinning like a maniac and murmuring, "Time ... to ... hi-ber-nate..."

Sybil was fighting it, but her eyes had rolled back in her head.

Wily could feel images crowding into his head – a warm den, a crackling fire, hot chocolate with marshmallows...

"Come on, lads, they've nearly gone," said Duncan. "Let's finish the job."

Wily put his hands in his pockets and pinched his legs, trying to stay awake. And in his right-hand pocket, he felt something. Something important.

He realized that it wasn't over yet.

He had a plan.

ENTER THE DRAGON

As Wily was rummaging through his pockets, he had found the pair of earplugs he'd been given on the aeroplane. The moment the skunks turned their backs, he whipped them out and stuck them up his nose – one in each nostril. Immediately his mind cleared and he snapped back to reality. He could hear the skunks hauling themselves up the rope into the Forbidden City, but he kept staring straight ahead, pretending to be in a trance.

As soon as they were out of the room, Wily leaped to his feet.

He shook Albert – there was no response.

He shook Sybil – she just stared into space and dribbled.

He grabbed Sybil's police radio.

"Julius! Julius!"

"Wily?"

"Call an ambulance. And get to the sewer beneath the Forbidden City."

"The sewer? What are you up to?"

"Just do it. And send your officers to the Forbidden City itself. It's an emergency."

"But – the Forbidden City – it'll take us half an hour to get there."

"As quickly as possible, then. Meanwhile, I'll do what I can."

Wily scrambled up the rope and into the Forbidden City.

He was in a side chamber in the eastern wing of the Emperor's old palace. All the lights were off, but he could still see mirrors glinting on the walls and chandeliers twinkling on the ceilings.

Wily breathed in and then remembered he had earplugs in his nostrils. Should he take them out? No, too risky. He'd have to forget his sense of smell and use his eyes and ears instead.

Wily listened and heard a scuffling sound in the room straight ahead. He darted forward and poked his head round the door. He could see a narrow balcony overlooking a large interior courtyard. The balcony was full of outfits and trinkets celebrating the Year of the Dragon. There were flags, banners, dragon costumes, drums, cymbals and more.

Down in the courtyard, Duncan and the skunks were prising open a cabinet that contained the world's biggest emerald.

Wily listened.

"We're going to get caught, boss. I know we are," gibbered Sam.

"No, we're not," snapped Duncan.

"I'm going to spray, I'm going to spray," stammered Sam.

"Spray all you like," said Duncan.

So Sam ejected a puff of white fizzy liquid out of his bottom.

Duncan pulled out his bottle of Utopia and poured a couple of drops on to the ground.

"All gone," he said.

"Why were you nervous, anyway?" asked Simon. "All the guards are gone."

"It's … it's … it's the ghost, OK? It's the ghost!" exclaimed Sam.

"What ghost?"

"The Ghost of the Jade Dragon. Everybody knows it protects the Beijing Emerald. Maybe we shouldn't steal it, after all."

Duncan glanced at the emerald. "There are no such things as ghosts," he hissed.

"Yeah, there are," said Sam. "After my great-great-grandmother died, she came back to me in the form of a wasp and stung me on the knee."

"That was just a wasp," said Duncan, wrenching the front off the cabinet and grabbing the jewel.

"Yeah, that was just a wasp," said Simon, but now he looked frightened.

Duncan put the emerald into a sack and moved on to the next cabinet.

"Please, put it back," said Sam. "Let's steal something else instead. There are lots of other jewels here."

"We're going to steal those, too," said Duncan. "We're going to take everything."

Wily moved silently to the other side of the balcony as Duncan started to crowbar the front off another cabinet. He had to stop them. By the time Julius arrived, Duncan and the skunks would have taken everything in the Forbidden City and vanished.

What could he do? There were three of them

– and Duncan had a heavy crowbar. He also wasn't sure how good the earplugs were. They were protecting him from Utopia and skunk spray up on the balcony, but what about at close range?

Wily closed his eyes, desperately trying to think of a solution.

"The dragon's ghost is here, I can sense it," Sam stammered. "I'm going to spray again."

And then Wily had an idea. He began rummaging through the trinkets on the balcony. Behind him was a huge papier-mâché dragon costume, complete with bulging eyes, flappy mouth and long tail. If one of the skunks was scared of a dragon ghost, perhaps Wily could take advantage of it.

But that wasn't all. Wily was still in his baggy red costume. Strapped to his back was a fire-eater's torch. If he positioned everything correctly, maybe his dragon could breathe fire, too.

He looked around for other props. Drums, cymbals – they could be useful. He picked up a waste-paper basket from the corner of the room, emptied it and knocked out the bottom. Now he had a megaphone.

In less than a minute, Wily was inside the dragon costume, holding the torch in front of his mouth. He held the megaphone in his other hand and attached the cymbals to his knees.

The skunks had opened a second cabinet and Duncan had removed the jewel – a giant diamond.

This was Wily's chance. He shouted through his megaphone: "Who dares remove my treasure?"

Sam Skunk immediately sprayed, yelling: "I told you! I told you! It's the ghost! It's the ghost!"

"Don't be ridiculous," said Duncan, "we must

have missed one of the guards. Come out, come out, wherever you are."

He held up his crowbar and the bottle of Utopia.

"I AM one of the guards," said Wily, and he brought his legs together, making the cymbals clash. "I guard the Beijing Emerald. And I protect it with fire!"

He leaped down from the balcony, the dragon's tail snaking behind him.

He opened the dragon's flappy mouth and turned on his fire-eater's torch.

"Sam, you were right!" cried Simon Skunk, and he sprayed, too.

"Calm down, it's one of the guards," said Duncan and he opened the bottle of Utopia, waving it at the dragon.

Wily couldn't smell anything – the earplugs in his nose were still working.

"Why do you wave perfume at me?" shouted Wily. "Is this any way for a skunk to fight?"

For the first time Duncan looked afraid. "B-but
… it should knock you out…" he stammered.

At that moment, Wily breathed on his
fire-eater's torch and a huge flame shot across
the room.

"Aaargh!" cried Duncan and, in spite of
himself, he sprayed.

Wily breathed fire again, sending a column
of flame up towards the ceiling.

"Put back what you have stolen!" he yelled.

"OK, w-we w-will," stammered Duncan. He tossed the diamond into the cabinet behind him. Then he sprinted across the room, took the emerald out of his sack and put that back, too.

"Now leave this place and never return!" boomed Wily, clashing the cymbals together again.

As Duncan scrambled towards the door, he knocked against the doorframe and his nose peg fell off.

"Oh no!" he cried, breathing in Utopia. "Sam, give me your peg!"

He grabbed Sam's nose peg, but Sam swiped it back and before long, all three skunks were coughing and stumbling and fighting for each other's pegs.

"It's ... too ... much..." coughed Duncan, and sank to his knees.

Sam and Simon coughed for a second and

they too fainted, then they began to grin and dribble.

Wily took off his dragon costume and looked at the three burbling skunks.

"Solving crime in record time," he murmured, with a smile.

He grabbed the cord from a pair of curtains and tied up the skunks. Then he reached inside the pocket of Duncan's jacket and pulled out a slip of paper.

The recipe for Utopia.

In Milan, Wily Fox was visiting Adolfo Aroma in his office. He handed back the recipe.

"Thank you, Mr Fox," said Adolfo. He crumpled the paper into a ball, popped it in his mouth and swallowed it. "Goodbye, Utopia, forever."

"A wise decision," said Wily.

"Now, tell me about your friends," said Adolfo, "the little squirrel and the mole. Have they recovered?"

"They're OK," said Wily. "The doctors found you can get Utopia out of your system quickly if you sit in a wind tunnel for a few hours. Blows it out of your lungs and nostrils and ears. Their hair looks weird, but they're fine."

"And those horrible skunks?"

"All in prison. The guards wear gas masks so they can't get knocked out by the skunks' spray."

"Very sensible," said Adolfo. "You know, I can't thank you enough, Mr Fox. This case could have destroyed my business. Ruined my life."

"All part of the service," said Wily.

"Well, if there's anything I can do for you, just name it," said Adolfo.

Wily thought for a few seconds. "Hmm. I guess there is one thing."

"There is? What?" asked Adolfo.

"Can I have some of that Smellissimo aftershave?" asked Wily. "You know, 'for the fox-about-town'. You see, my fur is still covered in skunk spray and I have to meet my next client in two hours."

"Of course!" Adolfo pressed a button on his desk. "Is it going to be an exciting case?"

"Just the usual saving-the-world-in-twenty-four-hours stuff. Nothing I can't handle," said Wily.

"I look forward to reading about it in the papers," said Adolfo.

"Oh no, this is a top-secret mission," said Wily. "It won't be in the news."

"That's a shame," said Adolfo. "Well, maybe you can write a book about it. When it's all over."

"That's not a bad idea," said Wily. "If it's like this one, I should have quite a story to tell!"

ABOUT THE AUTHOR

Adam Frost writes children's books full of jokes,
animals, amazing gadgets – and ideally all three!
When he was young, his favourite book was Roald
Dahl's *Fantastic Mr Fox*, so writing about fantastic
foxes all day is pretty much his dream job. His
previous books include *Ralph the Magic Rabbit*
and *Danny Danger and the Cosmic Remote*.

www.adam-frost.com